Saturdays with GG

Dwayne J. Clark

ILLUSTRATIONS BY *Debbie Tilley*

For my grandkids now, and on the way — D.J.C.

The illustrations were rendered in watercolor on 140-lb Saunders Waterford hot press paper
The display type was hand-lettered by Debbie Tilley
The text type was set in Century Expanded
Art direction and design by Joy Chu
Manufactured by Thomson-Shore, Dexter, MI (USA); RMA592MS944, December, 2013

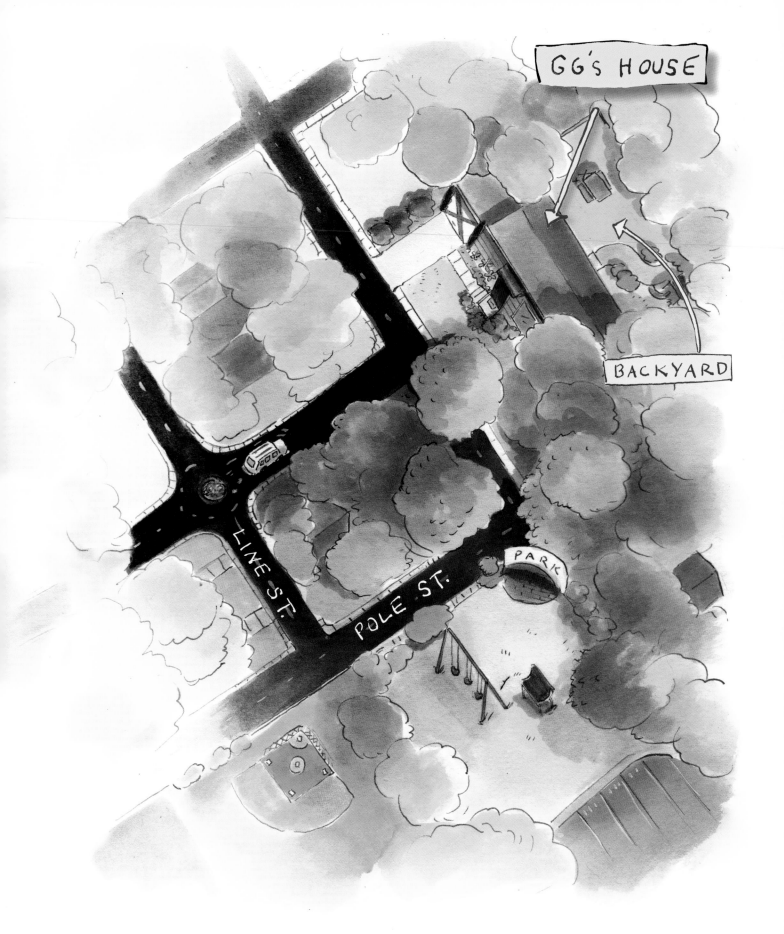

ANDRE AND HIS SISTER SOPHIA jumped out of their
mother's car and raced up the walk to Great Grandma's
house for their Saturday visit. GG, as they called her, and
their cousin Kennedy waved to them from the front porch.

"What are we going to do today, GG?" Andre asked.

"What would you like to do?" GG pulled each of them into a hug.

GG's big backyard was the perfect place to have adventures, and the children had lots of ideas.

"Play!" Sophia said.

"And put on a fashion show," Kennedy added.

"I'll be a pirate captain and sail the seas looking for ships to capture," Andre said. He was the oldest. He always came up with exciting games.

"Those are all wonderful ideas," said GG, "but first, how about helping me bake cookies?"

"Yay, cookies!" the children cheered.

GG's cookies were the best. In fact, everything GG baked was the best. Her favorite thing to do was to make delicious meals for the people she loved, and she was great at throwing parties.

"Peanut butter cookies?" Kennedy asked. Peanut butter was her favorite.

GG nodded. "We need flour, butter, eggs, sugar . . ." then her voice trailed off.

Kennedy carried the sugar.

Andre went to the refrigerator and grabbed a carton of eggs and the butter.

Sophia went to the pantry and got a bag of flour. She put it down and reached inside. "Glasses."

"There they are," GG said. "I thought I lost them. Thank you, Sophia, now I can read the recipe."

The children handed GG the ingredients one-by-one. She measured and mixed.

Andre eyed the big jar of peanut butter on a high shelf in the pantry—too high for him to reach. "What about the peanut butter?" he asked.

"I'll get it," GG said. "Why don't you scoot outside and play? I'll call you when the cookies are ready.

Andre, Sophia, and Kennedy ran outside. Andre zoomed to the picnic table as if he were an airplane.

Kennedy put a hand on her hip
and sashayed down the path. "I'd rather
play fashion show."

"Fashion show," Sophia mimicked.
"No fair. That's girl stuff," Andre grumbled.
"If you play fashion show with us, we'll
play spaceship with you later," Kennedy said.
"Okay," Andre agreed.
"This is my spaceship," he said,
climbing on top. "I'm the captain and
you can be my soldiers."
After staging a fashion show on the garden
path, Andre, Sophia, and Kennedy
zoomed through the
galaxy, searching
for space pirates.

GG opened the back door. "I've got fresh-baked cookies," she sang.

The children dashed inside. There was a plate of warm cookies and three glasses of ice-cold milk on the table.

Andre grabbed a cookie and took a big bite. Then his face fell. "These don't taste right."

Kennedy and Sophia both nibbled their cookies. Kennedy put hers down, but Sophia continued to eat. Then she took another. She left as many crumbs on the table as there were cookies on the plate!

Andre looked around. The flour, sugar, and eggs were still on the counter. Then he checked the pantry—the peanut butter was sitting on the top shelf. Andre took another bite of his cookie and realized what had gone wrong.

"GG, there isn't any peanut butter in your peanut butter cookies," he said.

"Of course there is," GG answered. "Peanut butter cookies always have peanut butter in them."

Kennedy didn't want to be rude, but she agreed with Andre. "These taste funny."

GG frowned and bit into a cookie herself. She chewed slowly. Then checked the pantry. "You're right, Andre and Kennedy. I forgot the peanut butter. How silly." She shook her head with a laugh.

Sophia grabbed another cookie. Half of it crumbled onto the table, but she popped the rest into her mouth. "I *like* it."

THE NEXT WEEKEND, all three children
arrived at GG's house for their Saturday visit.
After a round of hugs and kisses, she suggested
they go to the nearby park.

Sophia hopped up and down. "Swings!"

"Yes, swings," GG said.

They all held hands, and walked to the park.

Leaves floated to the ground in a
gentle breeze and gathered at
the base of a big oak tree.

"Look at the feathers falling," GG said.

Feathers? Andre thought. He looked at Kennedy but she only shrugged.

When they got to the park, Sophia ran to the swings. "Push?"

"C'mon children, climb on the highchairs and I'll give you all a push," GG said.

"I'll push Sophia," Andre said, but really he was thinking, *highchairs*? He gave Sophia a start on her swing while GG helped Kennedy, then he climbed onto a swing of his own and pumped his legs until he was flying higher and higher.

GG sat on a bench and watched the children swing, slide down the spiral slide, and climb the jungle gym. Soon it was time to go home.

"Let's go have a snack and then you can play in the backyard," GG said. "I'm making your favorite dinner—pot roast."

They were half way home when GG stopped on the corner and looked around. She gazed from one side of the street to the other. There were no cars coming, and Andre wondered why she was waiting.

"Aren't we going to cross the street, GG?" he asked.

GG nodded, but her eyes clouded over. "I just have to get my bearings."

"Your house is across the street and halfway down the block," he said quietly. *Why is GG being so weird?* he thought.

"I know where my house is," GG said quickly. "I just got turned around for a minute."

AFTER A SNACK of store bought cookies and milk, Kennedy and Sophia headed out to the backyard to play so that GG could make her pot roast. "Can I help, GG?" Andre asked.

"No thank you, Andre," she said. "Go and play."

Andre joined his sister and cousin in the backyard where they watched a string of ants carry crumbs to their nest. He soon forgot all about GG's strange behavior.

They were about to begin a game of hide and seek, when
he ran to the house to use the bathroom. "Be right back."

Kennedy took Sophia's hand. "Let's find a really good
hiding spot while he's inside."

"Yeah!" Sophia followed Kennedy behind the garden
shed.

Andre opened the back door expecting to find the
kitchen full of the delicious smells of GG's pot roast. Instead he
was met with the smell of smoke, and the kitchen was full of
gray haze. GG was asleep in her recliner in the living room.

A loud, high-pitched beep filled the air. The smoke alarm.

GG was startled out of her nap and ran into the kitchen.

"Why did you turn the oven on?" she asked.

She opened the back door to let the smoke out just as the
girls ran in to see what was wrong.

Andre stood on a chair and pressed a button on the smoke
alarm to make it stop beeping just like he had seen his father do at
home when he burned the toast.

GG turned to the three children. "I told you never to touch
the oven," she said. "It's very dangerous. You should know better."

Kennedy's eyes filled with tears. "We didn't, GG," she said.

Sophia's lower lip trembled. GG had never been mad at her before. She turned to her brother, confused.

"We didn't play with the oven," Andre said quietly. "You were making pot roast."

GG's eyes clouded over with a faraway look. Then she opened the oven door. The pot roast was black and burnt to a crisp.

GG shook her head. "I guess I fell asleep and forgot. She reached into the oven to remove the pan.

"Wait, GG!" Andre handed her a potholder. "Don't burn your hand."

GG put the blackened pan on the stove and kissed the top of Andre's head.

"I'm sorry I yelled at you," she said. "I know what good children you are."

Sophia and Kennedy each gave her a big hug. Then Sophia's stomach rumbled and everyone laughed.

"Okay, new plan," GG announced. "We'll have a picnic. You go outside and I'll make sandwiches."

Andre and Sophia ran outside to wipe off the picnic table, but Kennedy hung back. GG looked at the blackened pan and shook her head with a sigh.

"Can I help you make sandwiches, GG?" Kennedy asked.

GG gave herself a shake and then bustled to the pantry. "No thank you, Kennedy. Peanut butter and jelly sandwiches coming right up!"

"Don't forget the peanut butter," she said.

"Now why would I do that?" GG asked.

Kennedy didn't remind her that she had left the peanut butter out of the cookies the week before. She joined her cousins on the picnic table, and few minutes later GG came outside carrying a tray of peanut butter and jelly sandwiches and a pitcher of homemade lemonade. She even had slices of watermelon for dessert.

Lunch was delicious and fun. They had a watermelon-seed-spitting contest and GG won! Then she told wonderful stories about Fourth of July picnics she went to when she was a young girl. She and her father once won a three-legged race.

The children's grandparents, Papi and Bebe, picked them up at GG's house that night. Sophia and Kennedy had forgotten all about the burnt pot roast, but Andre was still troubled. GG wasn't herself, and he was worried.

After a flurry of hellos and goodbyes, the children climbed into Papi's car.

"Did you have a good time with GG today?" Bebe asked.

"GG's acting weird," Andre said. "She used wrong words for things and she got lost coming home from the park."

"Last week she forgot to put peanut butter in the peanut butter cookies," Kennedy added. "And this week we had cookies from the store. GG never buys cookies at the store."

"I *love* GG," Sophia said.

Andre turned to her. "I love GG, too, but today she scared me."

"GG's changing," Papi said. "She may not always be able to do things like bake cookies and take you to the park. But she loves you very much. There's nothing to be scared of."

"How is she changing?" Kennedy asked.

"Do you remember when we worked so hard last month mowing GG's lawn and pulling the weeds in the garden?" Papi asked. "We were all really tired afterward and wanted to rest, right?"

Sophia and Kennedy nodded.

"I was so tired I couldn't even think," Andre said.

"Exactly," Papi answered. "When your body gets tired, so does your mind. You forget things."

Andre was still feeling a little confused. "But GG didn't work hard today."

"Think of all the things GG has done for us over the years," Bebe said. "Remember when she had that circus party for your birthday, Kennedy, and she had clowns and ponies?"

"That was fun," Kennedy said.

Andre had won a science fair with GG's idea for a project. "She helped me make that cool volcano."

"GG's been working hard for years," Papi said. "Now she needs a rest, just like you did after we worked in the yard."

"But she didn't just forget things. She got mad and yelled at us, too," Kennedy said. "Andre's right. It was scary."

Bebe reached over the seat and took Kennedy's hand. "Sometimes as people get older, they may do things that aren't like them, but you don't have to be afraid. When she acts in a way that confuses you, try to be gentle and understanding."

"We need to do more for her now," Papi said. "You're all growing up, and you're ready to help her do things like take care of her yard and help her cook and things like that."

Andre was still troubled. "But GG fell asleep and burned the pot roast today. There could have been a fire. Who's going to help GG when we're not there?"

"We're going to make sure GG is safe," Papi said. "Everyone in the family will take a turn. Things are going to change, and GG may not be able to live alone for much longer, but I promise you that we'll do everything we can to keep her safe."

"I want to help," Andre said.

"Me, too," Kennedy and Sophia added.

"What can we do?" Andre asked.

"There are lots of things," Papi said. "Let's make a list."

GG, like many older people, suffers from dementia, or memory loss. There are many things that kids can do to make things easier and still have fun with the people they love. Papi and Bebe helped Andre, Kennedy, and Sophia make a list. These are things that you can do with your older friends and relatives, too.

1. Photographic Memories: Get out some old pictures and scrapbooks and ask your loved one to tell you all about what he or she was doing and what life was like when they were your age. What modern invention has made the biggest difference in their lives?

2. Cookie Contest: Help your loved one bake his or her favorite cookies. Read the recipe, line up the ingredients, and help mix the batter. Then bake your favorite cookie recipe. Invite your family to name the winner of the Best Cookie Contest. Be sure another adult is around to turn on the oven and to make sure the cookies don't burn.

3. Pets to the Rescue: Bring your puppy or kitten for a visit and tell your loved one all about your pet. Who doesn't like to spend time with furry friends?

4. Author! Author! Write a story about all the fun things you and your loved one do together, and draw pictures to go with it. Read it together on your next visit, or read your favorite picture book and talk about why you like it so much.

5. Rock Concert: Play your favorite music and pretend you're a pop star while you sing and dance for your grandma or grandpa. Then play some of his or her favorite songs and have a sing-along.

6. Let's go to Work: Think about what your grandma or grandpa did for a living. Find some props to help you talk to them about it, and pretend to do their job.

There's more! ☞

7. Now Playing: Pop some popcorn, gather your favorite movie snacks, and watch an old movie together. What was your grandma or grandpa doing when the movie first came out? Did he or she have a favorite movie star?

8. Top Chef: Ask a grown-up to help you prepare a favorite food based on an old family recipe. Over your meal, talk about the last time you ate this dish together and how the recipe came into the family.

9. Living in Luxury: Have a special spa day. Foot rubs, manicures and pedicures, and combing each other's hair are all things you could enjoy with your loved one. Just holding hands is a nice thing to do, too.

10. Puzzles and Games: Many older people like simple games and puzzles like Bingo, Go Fish, and word search games. Small jigsaw puzzles are fun, too. You can even have a favorite family photo turned into a puzzle for the two of you to do together.

11. Runway Models: Get out some fun jewelry and your favorite dress up costumes and put on a fashion show. What kinds of clothes did your grandma or grandpa wear when they were your age?

12. Scrapbook Fun: Create a new scrapbook of you with your loved one. Make sure to include photographs and your own pictures of the fun things you've done together and write captions to go along with them. Leave some blank pages in the back so that you can add even more memories.

Once Andre, Kennedy, and Sophia had some ideas for things they could do to help GG, they felt much better.

"Next Saturday I'm going to read GG my favorite book," Andre said. "It's about pirates!"

"Maybe Sophia and I could play music and ask GG to dance," Kennedy said.

Sophia clapped. "Dance party. I *love* GG!"

Resources

Want to learn more about Alzheimer's disease and dementia? Here are some **resources for families**:

Alzheimer's Association
www.alz.org
(800) 272-3900

Department of Heath and Human Services website for families facing Alzheimer's
http://www.alzheimers.gov
(877) 696-6775

Alzheimer's Foundation of America
http://www.alzfdn.org
(866) 232-8484

Alzheimer's Disease Education and Referral Center
http://www.nia.nih.gov/alzheimers/
(800) 222-2225

My Mother My Son
By Dwayne J. Clark
mymothermyson.com

Resources for Kids and Teens

The Alzheimer's Association has special information just for kids and teens:
http://www.alz.org/living_with_
alzheimers_just_for_kids_and_teens.asp

So does the **National Institute on Aging**:
http://www.nia.nih.gov/alzheimers/
alzheimers-disease-information-children-
and-teens-resource-list

This book is lovingly dedicated to
MARY COLLEEN CALLAHAN CLARK
Mom, Gram, and GG

— D.J.C.